Contents

1   Major Konrad   1

2   School   9

3   Strike   19

4   In the Woods   23

5   In Hiding   29

6   Resistance   35

7   Elli   43

8   Hunger   51

9   Suspicion   57

10 Arrested   65

11 Hitler's Dead   71

12 The Truth is Told   79

Chapter 1
Major Konrad

"Check mate," said Major Konrad. "I've beaten you at chess again, Bakker. You need to think what you are doing."

"I could never beat you at chess, Major. You are too good for me. You would be a world grandmaster if there wasn't a war on."

This made Jan angry. He had been watching his father and the Major finish their game. He knew that his father could beat the German officer any time. But he just let him win.

Jan knew why his father did this. The Bakkers were Dutch and the Germans had invaded Holland. Jan's father worked for the Germans. He was in the Nazi Police. The Major could help him. It was worth being nice to him.

Jan's mother slammed the kettle down on the stove. She was angry too.

"Are you making coffee, Mrs Bakker?" asked Major Konrad.

"Yes," she said. "Not real coffee, of course. This is the awful stuff we Dutch have to drink. It's made from acorns and things. Would you like a cup?"

"Ah, but I have something for you," he said with a smile, and pulled a small package out of his pocket. "Some real coffee as a little gift from the German government."

Jan's mother took the package. She said nothing. Soon the room was full of the rich smell of real coffee. He longed for some. His mother took the boiling kettle off the stove and went to get cups from the shelf. She only got two cups.

"Aren't you having any, Mrs Bakker?" asked Major Konrad.

"No, Major, it will only keep me awake. Now off to bed, Jan, it's school tomorrow."

"But, Mother," said Jan, as she pushed him out of the kitchen, "I love coffee, you know I do. And so do you."

"No-one else in Holland is drinking real coffee just now. So we can do without it too," she told him. There was anger in her voice. "Now go to bed." She gave him a kiss.

Jan lay in his bed and shivered. It was cold outside and there was very little coal to heat the houses. *I wish all this was over*, he thought. *I wish the Germans would get out of Holland so that things could get back to normal.* He remembered what fun life had been before the war, and smiled.

Outside he could hear Major Konrad leaving. Jan looked out.

"Heil Hitler!" cried Major Konrad, raising his arm in the Nazi salute.

"Heil Hitler!" replied Jan's father, and raised his arm.

Jan looked across the street and saw people watching from their windows. He got back into bed. *Even when this awful war is over*, he thought, *it won't be over for us. Everyone hates us.*

It was like this all the time. Jan wished his father wasn't helping the Germans.

Chapter 2
School

"Jan!" shouted his mother. "Hurry up. You know how angry Miss Hals gets if you're late for school."

Jan picked up his bag but he didn't hurry. School was hell these days. He set off sadly down the road, walking very slowly.

He waited for something bad to happen. It didn't take long. A boy in his class, Pieter, came up beside him.

"And how did you enjoy your *real* coffee last night?" he asked.

"I didn't drink any coffee," Jan told him.

Another boy, Willem, came up on the other side of Jan. "Oh, so it was just Mummy and Daddy drinking coffee with the nice German officer, was it?" he mocked.

Then Willem grabbed Jan's bag and flung it over a fence. The three boys watched the bag as it flew through the air and landed near the canal.

"Why are you doing this? You used to be my friends," said Jan.

"That was before your dad started helping the Germans and before my dad was sent away to a work camp in Germany," said Willem.

"It's a pity the bag didn't fall into the canal," said Pieter. "Then Miss Hals would have been really angry."

Jan got over the fence and picked up his bag. *I'll be late for school again*, he thought. But he didn't mind.

He hated school these days. No-one spoke to him. It had got worse now that the other children's fathers had been taken away. No-one knew if they were alive or dead. That was why the other children hated Jan so much. *His* father was not going to be sent to Germany.

****

Just as he got to school, the town clock struck eight.

"Late again, Jan Bakker," said Miss Hals crossly. "Third time in a week. You will have to stay behind after school and clean up as a punishment. It won't be so bad. You'll have a nice, hot cup of *real* coffee waiting for you when you get home."

"Mother and I didn't drink any of that coffee," Jan told her angrily. "Mum says if no-one else in Holland can have coffee, then we won't drink it either."

"I see," said Miss Hals. "Well, well. But you will have to stay in after school, Jan, anyway. You've been late too often."

Jan sat at the back of the room as he always did.

No-one spoke to him. No-one looked at him. It was as if he wasn't there.

Then the door opened and Elli Wessel came in. Her eyes were red. It was a surprise to see her at all.

Elli hardly ever came to school any more. She was always off sick.

Is it because her father, like my father, is in the Nazi Police? thought Jan. She was bullied by the other children too.

As Elli walked through the class to the back of the room, all the others looked down at their desks, as if she wasn't there.

Elli sat down next to Jan. He put his hand on her arm.

Elli smiled at him, dried her eyes and wrote him a note:

I can't stand the silence any more.
No-one will talk to me.

Jan wrote back:

I know. I feel the same, but be brave.
We haven't done anything wrong and the
war will be over soon.

Elli wrote back:

It will never be over for us. People
will never forgive anyone who was
on the side of the Nazis.

"What's this?" Miss Hals was standing
over them. "You two have been writing
notes to each other." She grabbed the paper
and read it.

"Oh dear," she said sadly, "your fathers
help the Nazis and you pay the price.

The rest of us don't understand how hard it must be for you, Jan and Elli."

Chapter 3
Strike

After school, Jan followed Elli out of the building. "Shall I walk home with you?" he asked.

"Why?" she said.

"To make sure you get home safely. And so you'll have someone to talk to."

"It's awful, isn't it?" said Elli. "By not speaking to us, they tell us how much they hate us."

When Jan got home, his father was banging his fist on the table and shouting at his mother. "They're crazy, I tell you, they're crazy! No good will come of this."

"What's this all about?" asked Jan.

"All the railway men are going on strike. The trains won't go at all in Holland."

"Why?" asked Jan.

"So the Germans can't move men and guns around."

"What will happen to the railway men?" asked Jan.

"They'll be sent to prison," his father told him. "And the leaders may be shot."

"What else will the Germans do?" asked Jan.

"They are going to cut off all our coal and food," said his mother. "It will be a long, hard winter. We shall have no heat or light and very little food."

"What will we do?" asked Jan.

"We'll have to get wood from the forests and food anywhere we can," his mother told him. "The farmers won't give *us* any food. Everyone knows that your father is on the side of the Germans. It's going to be a *very* hard winter for us. Unless the Major brings us more of his little presents."

Chapter 4
In the Woods

It got harder and harder to get food to eat or wood for the fire. Everyone was hungry and cold. At school, the children wore all the clothes they had. The older boys had gone. Some had been sent to work in Germany. Others were in hiding.

Every day and night, British and American planes flew over the town on their way to bomb Germany.

"The war must be over soon," Jan said to Elli one day when they were looking for wood in the forest.

"My mother listens to the London radio. They say the Americans and the British have landed in France. They'll soon be here," she told him.

"It's a crime to listen to the London radio," Jan said. "Take care."

"The Germans don't worry about *our* families," Elli told him. "After all, our fathers have joined the Nazi Police."

"So, that makes you and I Nazi-lovers too, does it?" asked Jan.

"Well, does it?" said Elli. She turned and looked at him hard. "Do you want the Germans to win this war? They bomb our towns, they take away our men and our food and put anyone who is against them in prison or shoot them. How do *you* feel, Jan?"

Jan was thinking hard. "You're right, Elli. I hate the Germans. Our fathers made a stupid and wicked choice. They joined the Nazis. But this doesn't mean that we have to do the same thing, does it?"

"No, Jan, but what can we do about it?"

"Nothing," said Jan sadly. "The Dutch Resistance would not have us. They'd think we might betray them to the Germans."

"That's right," agreed Elli, "but we can fight the Nazis in our own way."

"What do you mean?" asked Jan. "I don't understand."

"Just think a moment," said Elli. "Which children in our class know things that would be useful to the Resistance?"

"We do," said Jan in surprise.

"Right. When Major Konrad and the other Nazis come to our house, they tell my father all sorts of things."

"Yes!" cried Jan. "And my father often tells my mother what the German plans are. But, Elli, we can't tell these things to the Resistance because they would not believe or trust us. So who *can* we tell?"

"We'll have to work that one out," said Elli.

Just then, they saw an old and empty hut behind some trees. The door was hanging open and the roof had fallen in. They stopped and stared.

"Did you know there was an empty hut here in the woods?" said Jan.

Elli shook her head. "Hush, it's not empty at all. Look – someone is coming out."

Chapter 5

In Hiding

Jan and Elli hid behind a tree and watched. A man and a girl came out, very thin, their clothes torn and old. They were picking things up off the ground.

"They're looking for mushrooms," said Jan.

As they got nearer, Jan took a sharp breath. Elli looked at him but said nothing.

As soon as the pair were out of sight, Elli asked, "Who are they? Do you know them?"

"Of course I do. It's Dr Stein, our dentist, and his daughter Ruth, who used to be in our class."

"I didn't live here then," Elli said. "Are they Jews?"

Jan nodded, "Yes, they went away. People said they had gone to England or America."

"There will be a reward for anyone who tells the Germans where they are. The Nazi Police offer lots of money to people who betray Jews."

"Elli, what are you thinking?"

"No, of course I'm not going to betray them. But more and more people come here now to look for food and wood. The Steins will be found out."

Just then, they heard the sound of voices and hid behind some bushes.

"Dr Stein, you mustn't go out into the woods. It's not safe," said a voice they knew. "I've got you some milk and a bit of fish and bread. It's not much, but it's the best I can do. We're all hungry now."

Jan began to shake. It was Pieter – the boy from his class who bullied him. Pieter's father had been shot for being in the Resistance. And he was now risking his own life by hiding and feeding Jews.

"You're right, Pieter," said Dr Stein. "But we need some fresh air and mushrooms and roots to eat."

"But you can't risk your life and Ruth's too. The war must end soon. The British and

Americans are in France. They've got as far
as the south of Holland. Just wait a bit
longer."

"We're very grateful to you, Pieter. But we can't stand living in this old hut much longer," said Ruth.

"Look – I've got some books for you," Pieter told her. "And here's a pack of cards. It's the best I can do. Stay here till it gets dark. Then, go to the Groots' farm. There you can get warm and get some sleep and hot food."

"And have a bath?" asked Ruth with a smile.

"There's no hot water any more," Pieter told her.

"It gets worse and worse," said Ruth.

"I know," grinned Pieter. "But the war's nearly over now."

"People have been saying that for months." Ruth shook her head.

"Yes, but this time it's true," said her father. "Look at the British and American planes that go over us. They're bombing Germany. Soon the Nazis will have to give in."

Chapter 6
Resistance

Jan sat in the kitchen and ate his carrot and potato soup.

"It's the best I can do," said his mother. "You can't get meat or bread anywhere. Just be grateful it's hot. When our coal runs out you'll be eating cold food."

Just then, Jan heard the sound of an axe. He ran to the window and saw his father in the garden, cutting down their apple tree.

"Dad, no!" he yelled. "I love that tree! I used to swing on it when I was little. And we can eat the apples."

"Too bad," his father yelled back. "We need to keep warm. You can't get upset about a tree these days. Come and help me. Major Konrad will be here very soon."

"I'll just finish my soup," called Jan. He ate it as slowly as he could. Soon he heard the sound of a motorbike, and Major Konrad strode in.

Jan's father came in from the garden.

"We need you now, Bakker. We have been told that there are young men hiding in the woods near the old hut. They could be Resistance fighters or Jews. Come to us at twelve. We're going to search every bit of those woods and we'll need all the men we can get."

Jan began to hum as if he had heard nothing.

"See you at twelve, Major. Heil Hitler!" cried Jan's father.

"Heil Hitler!" replied the Major.

Jan was thinking fast. "Mum, I feel sick. I can't help Dad with the tree right now."

"All right, Jan," said his mother. She put a hand on his head. "You do feel hot. You'd better lie down for a bit."

Jan let his mother tuck him up in bed.

As soon as she had gone, he grabbed a scrap of paper and wrote on it:

They are going to search the woods near you today. Go and hide on the other side of the river.
A friend

Then he got up, climbed out of his
window and ran to the woods. When he got
near to the old hut, he stopped and hid
behind a tree. He picked up a stone.

He wrapped the note round the stone and threw it at the window. The glass smashed. *They must have heard it*, Jan thought, and he turned round and ran home before anyone saw him.

Jan climbed back into his room through the window. His heart was thumping. *Will they find the note?* he thought. *Did I get there in time?*

When his mother came up with more soup on a tray, he told her he was feeling better. "I'd rather eat at the table," he said. Then he would hear any news.

Jan sat in the kitchen all day, waiting for news. He was scared.

At last his father came in and slammed the door. *They didn't find them*, thought Jan, *or he'd be in a better mood.*

"We searched all afternoon in that freezing forest and found nothing," Jan's father said.

"Well, I'm glad you got so cold. You were hunting people like animals. You should be ashamed," his wife told him.

"But they're not people – Jews and Resistance fighters are rats," he replied. "Anyway, someone had been living in the hut. There were still the remains of a fire and food in there."

"Maybe someone warned them," said Jan's mother.

"No way," said his father. "Only the Germans and the Police knew we were going to search the woods."

Jan pretended to be asleep.

"Anyway, whoever was in that old hut has got away for now," said his father.

Chapter 7
Elli

On the way to school the next day, Jan saw Elli. He ran to catch up with her. "Hey, Elli, I did it," he told her, smiling.

"What did you do?" Elli asked.

"I was in the kitchen yesterday when Major Konrad came to tell my dad that they were going to search the woods. I went and told the Steins."

Elli stopped and looked at him with huge eyes. "You told them?"

Jan nodded.

"I wrote a note. I didn't say it was from me. I wrapped it round a stone and chucked it through the window."

"Jan, that was *so* clever. I'm *so* proud of you."

"Look at the lovebirds," came Pieter's voice.

"Jan loves Elli, Jan loves Elli," the others sang.

"Don't listen to them," Elli told Jan. But she blushed a deep red. Then she took his arm. Jan saw that she held her head high for the first time that he could remember.

"We need a plan. Let's meet after school."

So after school, he went over to Elli's house.

"Be back before dark," said his mother. "We don't want the Germans to arrest you for being out late."

"You're a bit young to be going out with girls, aren't you?" said his father.

"Don't tease him. He needs friends," said Mrs Bakker. "It's hard on Jan and me to be hated by everyone because you're a Nazi-lover. No-one will talk to us. Elli is the only friend Jan has at the moment. So leave him alone."

Jan smiled at his mother and ran out of the door.

He didn't see a gang of boys coming
towards him. One of them put out his foot
and tripped Jan up. He fell flat on his face
in the hard snow. The other boys laughed as
Jan got to his feet and limped on to Elli's
house.

When he got there, Elli took him up to
the bathroom and washed the blood off his
hands and elbows.

"I wish it was all over, Elli," said Jan. "It just goes on and on."

"But, Jan, don't you see? It's good. If the others bully us like this, no-one else is going to suspect what we're doing. Now that you've begun to make use of what you hear at home, the Germans might suspect us. If we are still being bullied, no-one will find out that we've changed sides."

"You're so clever, Elli," said Jan. "Have you heard anything new today?"

Elli shook her head, "No, nothing. The Nazis are very angry because they searched the woods all day and found no-one. They have no new plans at the moment."

"I think the Germans know that things are going badly for them. The British or American soldiers will be here in a few weeks or months."

"I know," agreed Elli. "But we must try and see that no-one else gets killed before they get here."

"We're part of the Resistance, aren't we, Elli?" smiled Jan. "In our own way."

"We are," she smiled back. "We are. There's only two of us, but we're playing a very important part."

Chapter 8
Hunger

Jan's family sat close to the tiny log fire. The cooking pot hung over it. They were all tucked up in blankets.

They had no gas, no electricity and very little coal or food.

"Your friends the Germans keep punishing us all the time," said Jan's mother. "We have so little food that some people are slowly starving to death."

"Don't start that again," replied her husband.

"At least we still have something to eat," Jan's mother said, as she handed him a plate with a few potatoes. There was something else floating in the water.

"What's this, Mum?" asked Jan.

"Your mother is giving us tulip bulbs to eat," said his father. "That's all we can get."

Jan made himself eat the soup. It was awful.

Just then a German called Private Stern came in with a very young soldier. "Sorry to bother you, Bakker, but the Major wants you at Nazi Head Office."

Jan hoped he could find out what was going on.

"Is it something important?" he asked Private Stern.

"No, Jan, they're just arresting some more people."

Then he turned to Jan's mother. "I am sorry but we have orders to search every house. We are looking for Resistance fighters and fit young men who are in hiding so they won't be taken off to German work camps," said Private Stern.

"But my husband is in the Nazi Police. You can't suspect us of hiding anyone," said Jan's mother.

"My orders are to search every house in the town. Even stupid orders have to be carried out."

"Go on then. We've nothing to hide," she replied.

While the two soldiers were searching, Jan raced over to Elli's house.

"Elli, the Germans are searching every house in the town."

"We know who's working against the Germans," cried Elli. "We'll push notes under their doors to warn them and then ring the bell and run."

"And no-one will know it was us," said Jan.

As fast as they could, Jan and Elli wrote the notes and posted them, ringing on doorbells and then running away as they had planned.

Chapter 9
Suspicion

Spring came and it got warmer. But still there was very little food and everyone looked thin and ill.

Sometimes the Germans gave Jan's father a bit of meat. It was cooked in a thick soup with potatoes and carrots and had to last for days.

Major Konrad came to eat with them one evening, bringing with him some oranges.

Jan decided he hated Major Konrad so much he wouldn't eat an orange.

"Yes, you Dutch are being very difficult," Major Konrad said, "and there is a traitor somewhere among you. We must find him and punish him."

"What do you mean?" said Jan's father.

"You know, Bakker. Every time we try to find the Resistance fighters and the Jews, they've gone. Someone is warning them."

Jan was scared. "Do you know who it is?" he asked.

"I think so," replied the Major. "Have an orange, Jan, they're good."

Shaking, Jan took the orange. If the Major thought he was the traitor, it was not a good idea to refuse his gift.

As soon as he could, Jan rushed over to Elli's house. "Major Konrad knows that people are being warned when a search is coming," he told her. "He says he thinks he knows who it is."

"Does he think it's *you*?" asked Elli.

"I think so," nodded Jan.

"You must be careful. I'll deliver the notes alone from now on."

"They may suspect you too," Jan pointed out. "The risk is the same for both of us."

"No, it isn't," said Elli. "I'm a girl and everyone in this town thinks I'm a wimp. I heard my father talking on the phone today and there is something we have to do at once."

"What?" demanded Jan.

"We have to go and warn Pieter that the Police are coming to arrest him today. They know he's part of the Resistance."

"Good," said Jan. "I hate Pieter. He's made my life miserable for years. I'm not going to risk my life for him." And he went towards the door.

Elli stood between Jan and the door. "Jan, stop it," she yelled. "You sound like a Nazi. Just remember we're on the side of the Resistance."

"But, Elli, Pieter has bullied you too. How can you care what happens to him?"

"Because he's a human being. Of course he's angry with the Germans. His father was shot, remember? Of course he hates us. He thinks we're on the same side as his father's killers."

Jan blushed. "You're right, Elli. But it's very hard to care about people who hate you."

"I know," agreed Elli. "Now, you write the note and I'll go out and chuck it through Pieter's window."

Jan wrote in capital letters:

GET OUT! THE POLICE ARE COMING FOR YOU TONIGHT!

"Good," said Elli. "Now give it to me and go home." Elli ran down the street with the note in her pocket.

Jan set out for home. Then he thought to himself, *I must make sure she's all right. I'll follow her.*

Jan followed Elli through the empty streets until they came to Pieter's house. Jan could see Pieter's mother through the window.

Elli picked up a stone, wrapped the note round it and threw it at the window, which broke.

But to his horror, Jan saw that the note had dropped off and blown across the street. Jan ran to fetch it. He tore it into tiny bits.

Just then, the door of the house flew open and Pieter's mother rushed out. Elli ran, but the woman was too fast for her and grabbed her.

"You little Nazi-lover," she shouted. "Smashing people's windows!"

Jan ran up, "It's all my fault," he told the angry woman. "I told her to do it. Your Pieter has made us both miserable for too long. I'm glad the Germans are coming for him today."

Pieter's mother went white when Jan said that. She ran back into the house.

"Well, we gave her the message," said Elli, smiling.

"But we're in a mess now," Jan replied.

Chapter 10
Arrested

Elli and Jan walked back to Jan's house. Jan's mother was at the door waiting for them, in tears.

"How could you two do that?" she shouted. "People hate us anyway. This war will be over any day now and we've been on the wrong side."

Elli and Jan looked at each other and thought, *We haven't been on the wrong side.*

"Why did you smash that window?" Jan's mother went on.

"It wasn't Jan, it was me," Elli told her.

"But I told her to do it," added Jan.

Just then, there was a knock at the door. It was Private Stern.

"Sorry, Mrs Bakker, but I've been told I've got to bring these two children into Nazi Head Office. There are a few questions we need to ask them. In fact, they've done something bad."

"What – smashed a window?"

"We have to keep up law and order. Come on, Elli and Jan, this won't take long."

As the three of them walked to the Police Station, Jan asked, "What's going to happen to us?"

"You'll have to wait and see," he replied. "Now listen, you two. I know what you've been up to and I don't blame you. I'd have done the same myself. This awful war is almost over. It will only be a few days now. There's no point in more killing. So just say you're sorry. Tell them you didn't mean to do it. Then go home and stay there till it's all over. Don't try to be heroes, OK?"

"Why are you helping us?" asked Elli. "We're not on the same side."

"Oh yes we are," said Private Stern. "We're longing for this hell to be over. Now, don't say anything and I won't betray you. Let's all pray to God that it's over soon."

Elli and Jan stared at Private Stern.

"Don't be surprised. Germans are not all monsters. I never agreed with Hitler and I never joined the Nazi Party. But Major Konrad's a real Nazi, so just be very polite. Tell him how sorry you are and pretend to be scared."

"I *am* scared," Jan told him.

"Good," nodded Private Stern, as they arrived at the Nazi Head Office. "Now remember, don't try to be heroes."

Chapter 11
Hitler's Dead

Jan and Elli sat outside Major Konrad's room for ages.

"He always does this," Jan told Elli. "Dad told me he does it just to make people even more scared."

"Well it works, doesn't it?" said Elli. "I'm shaking all over."

Then the door opened and there stood Major Konrad looking very angry. "All right, you two. You come in first, Miss Elli."

"Thank you, Major Konrad," said Elli and she walked into the room. The door slammed behind her.

Jan felt sick. He could hear Major Konrad shouting. *Is this just about a broken window*, thought Jan, *or does Major Konrad really know something?*

At last, Elli was pushed out of the room. Jan could see she had been crying. Then Major Konrad yelled, "All right, Jan Bakker, your turn now."

Jan stood with his head down, trying to look sorry.

"Right," said Major Konrad, "I know it all. You and Elli have been warning Jews and Resistance fighters. You told them

when we were going to conduct a search.
That's how they get away."

Jan thought, *Major Konrad is just saying
this. He knows nothing. Elli won't have told
him anything.*

"Oh, no," cried Jan. "Why would Elli and I do that? After all, our families are on *your* side."

"Well, the war won't last for ever. You may be afraid you backed the wrong side. You may want to make sure you won't be punished when we go back to Germany and leave you to face the Resistance."

Jan saw that Major Konrad didn't know the truth.

"Oh, no, Major, I don't feel like that at all. I mean, my father has been working for you all through the war. No-one in the Resistance would believe a word we said."

"That makes sense," said the Major. "But someone tipped off the Jews hiding in the hut. And someone told everyone that we were coming to search people's houses. If it's not you and Elli, who is it?"

"I don't know, Major," said Jan. "But whoever it is, I hope you find them soon."

"I will, don't worry, I will. Now, off you go and don't smash any more windows. I don't want Pieter's mother in here again. She's no friend of yours, I can tell you."

"No, sir. Well, I hate Pieter. He picks on Elli and me all the time. We wish you'd put him in prison, sir."

"Good. Well, off you go now."

Shaking all over, Jan walked through the Nazi Head Office. He passed a room where some soldiers were listening to the radio. Jan stopped for a moment and heard a voice saying, "Our great leader Adolf Hitler is dead. He died doing his duty. Long live Germany ..."

Jan saw that many of the soldiers were crying.

Yippee! The war is almost over, thought Jan, as he raced out into the street to find Elli and tell her the wonderful news.

Chapter 12
The Truth is Told

One moment the town was silent and then, a second later, everyone seemed to spill out onto the street.

"The Germans have lost the war!" they were shouting.

"The war is over!"

"The British are almost here ..."

"Peace at last!"

That night, a huge bonfire was lit in the town and the town band played. People danced and sang.

In Jan's small room, Jan and Elli listened to the music and sniffed the sweet smell of the bonfire.

"Come on, Jan," cried Elli. "Let's dance, just the two of us."

Then the music stopped.

"What is it?" asked Elli. They looked out of the window.

"Listen, it's tanks," cried Jan, "I can hear them."

"Are the Germans coming back?" asked Elli, feeling scared.

"No, it's the British. Everyone's cheering. Look – there's Pieter. He's sitting up on one of the tanks. They're British tanks – the British are here to set us free."

"Oh, Jan," said Elli, "this is the best moment of my life."

"Mine too," agreed Jan. "But remember, to everyone else, we're still the children of Nazi-lovers. They'll still hate us."

"I don't care," said Elli. "I know, and you know, that we did our bit to help the Resistance."

Then there was a loud knock at the door.

"It's the Dutch Police," Jan said.

"They must have come for your father," Elli replied.

"Jan," came his mother's voice, "come down at once."

Jan ran downstairs. His mother's face was pale and she was crying. "They've come to take your father away. Say goodbye to him."

Jan looked at his father, standing there in handcuffs, looking small and scared.

"Goodbye, Dad. Come back soon," he said and tried hard to smile.

"Bye, son, take care of your mother. Do your best. I'll be thinking of you."

"Enough of that, Bakker," said a police officer. "Think about all the men you handed over to the Germans. What happened to their wives and children? Now, move on, you creep. Prison's too good for you." Jan could see how much the officer hated his father. He knew he would not see his dad again for a long time.

****

Life went on the same for Jan and Elli. No-one would speak to them at school. Only Ruth, the daughter of the Jewish dentist, was kind. She was back in their class.

"It's not Elli's or Jan's fault that their fathers were Nazi-lovers," she told the others, "just as it wasn't my fault that my father was a Jew."

But no-one listened to her.

Then the news got round that Ruth and her family were going to leave and start a new life in America.

"Let's send her a good luck card," said Jan. "She's been so nice to us."

"Good idea," agreed Elli.

So Elli made a card and Jan wrote:

To our friend Ruth, the only one who tried to understand. Good luck!

They went down to the train station to give it to her.

The whole town was at the train station to say goodbye to the Steins. Jan and Elli had to push their way through the crowd to get to Ruth. Jan handed her the card. She opened it and a look of surprise came over her face.

"Jan," she said, "Jan Bakker, I've seen this writing before. So it was you who warned us that the Germans were going to search the woods. It *was* you. It was, wasn't it?"

Jan blushed.

"Was it you?" demanded Ruth and Dr Stein.

"Yes, it was Jan," shouted Elli. "He risked his life for you and lots of others."

"Not just me," said Jan, "Elli too. It was Elli who threw the stone through your window, Pieter."

"You were trying to warn us," said Pieter, amazed.

"We *did* warn you," said Elli.

"Let's get this right. Are you saying that you found out the German plans from your fathers and then warned us?" asked Pieter.

Jan and Elli nodded.

The train began to move.

"Jan and Elli, thank you, and God bless you," shouted Ruth as the train got up speed. "You were heroes. You saved our lives."

For a moment there was a silence in the crowd.

Then Pieter said, "Jan, Elli, would you like to come and have a coffee with me? I want to hear more."

"We'd love a coffee, thank you," they said.

"I think we should thank you for what you did for the Resistance," said Pieter. "We have treated you badly. Maybe now we can start to make up for it." Pieter put his arm around Jan's shoulders. "We may even end up being friends again."

Then the three of them ran off together, laughing, to catch up with the rest of their class.

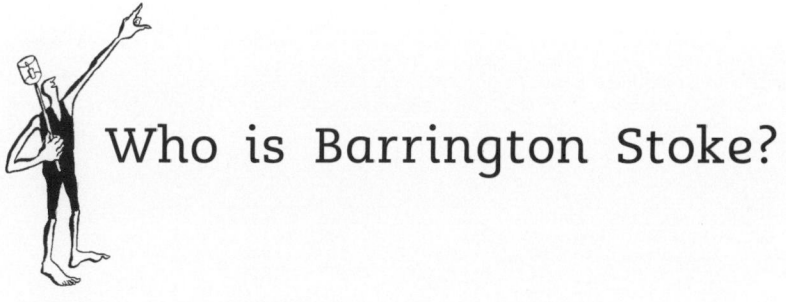

Who is Barrington Stoke?

Barrington Stoke went from place to place with his lamp in his hand. Everywhere he went, he told stories to children. Some were happy, some were sad, some were funny and some were scary.

The children always wanted more. When it got dark, they had to go home to bed. They went to look for Barrington Stoke the next day, but he had gone.

The children never forgot the stories. They told them to each other and to their children and their grandchildren. You see, good stories are magic and they can live for ever.

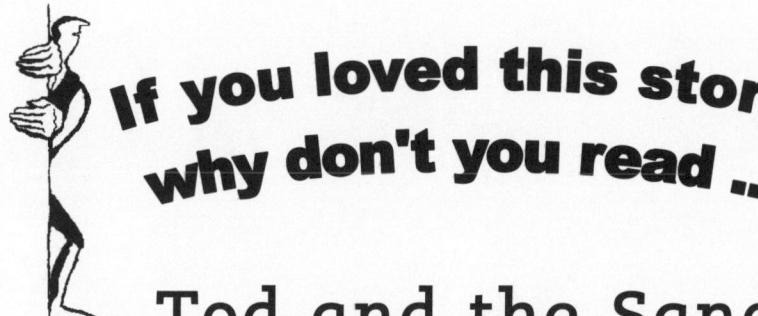

If you loved this story, why don't you read ...

Tod and the Sand Pirates

by Anthony Masters

Have you ever had to fight for your life? The whole world is suffering from a lack of water. Tod and Billy are looking for a new water supply, when pirates take them prisoner. How will they escape?

4u2read.ok!

You can order this book directly from our website
www.barringtonstoke.co.uk

If you loved this story, why don't you read ...

Hostage

by Malorie Blackman

Can you imagine how frightened you would be if you were kidnapped? Angela is held to ransom and needs all her skill and bravery to survive.

4u2read.ok!

You can order this book directly from our website
www.barringtonstoke.co.uk